THE UNSTOPPABLE
STOPMAN
ISSUE ONE

1

In Quad City U.S.A. the authorities take their security seriously.

At the main branch of the Quad City bank, which is downtown, two security guards are in an open safe. Next to them upon a table exists a huge mound of money. The money is substantial. It's the size of a miniature skyline.

"Guard this cash with your life." says one guard to the other.

"I'll devote my life to it."
replies the other.

As his partner leaves the safe, the man guarding the cash grabs the weaponry nearby on another table. He puts on his handgun, loads his machine gun, and spends careful time putting his knives in their chambers upon his bullet proof vest.

He spends this moment with his back turned away from the mountain of money.

Then, he finishes and turns his back.

The money is GONE, all of it.

His gives the look of a man with omelet on his face.

At a high-class party in the city's downtown, many celebrities local and worldly known walk this red carpet. A woman in gaudy and shiny jewelry and fur coat walks that rug. The paparazzi take photos of her; especially her expensive necklace.

Then, a squirrel emerges from that fur coat.

The furry animal crawls across her chest and snatches her diamond necklace.

She screams.

The squirrel runs across the red rug and disappears into the crowd. Cameras flash.

"Stop that squirrel!" says a security guard.

But to no avail. That animal's gone.

At a local favorite game show called "You bet your bills" host Ryan Evers asks a contestant a question.

"And now Daniela," Ryan says to the woman. "Here's the question to win this BRAND NEW CAR!

Sure enough it is a beautiful new model. The model is next it on a stage, while the game is right next to them.

The studio audience is transfixed. Ryan reads the question.

   "Okay, what day does the bill
for the water get paid at
Gerald's home?"

	The studio shows a picture
of a man not shaved and uncouth,
looking at the audience. It
hovers above that new car.

	"hmm." says the lady
contestant. "He doesn't pay,
because he's been broke all
month?"

	Ryan looks to the card. He
smiles.

"That's right, Daniela!" says the host. "You win the car!"

Daniela the contestant screams, along with the studio audience.

She goes to hug Ryan Evers.

He barely hugs back.

"Watch the suit, please." he says with a fake smile.

She then goes to claim her prize, walking across stage.

Then, the game show's mascot, a yellowish-white dog named Spencer emerges inside on the driver's seat. It stuns the contestant and everyone else.

The then dog starts the car, and speeds off-stage.

On the studio lot, the security guards try to stop the driving dog. Spencer signals a right-turn with his paw. He then confronts a blockade, made by the desperate guards. However, the clever canine jumps that car over it; escaping into the night.

QCBF News also reports:

"Many animals have broken out of the many locations of Quad City's biggest pet stores." speaks a female newscaster on television. "Bark O' Down, a man who literally wears a hound dog's mask...all the time, is now begging for the help of STOPMAN; for he is suspicious of different materials missing throughout the city, and fears loss of his. Many men pretending to be the Unstoppable Stopman have approached him, but have been refuted."

2

Sean Paus is still the same friendly *Stop Store* cart-pusher. He's been holding a tired look recently. It is both from the work he gets paid for, and the thankless job of being a hero.

At the front of the massive department store he is on the payphone with his friend Malcolm Criss. Malcolm is now on job release sentence in the Quad County Jail. He's in for resisting arrest. He disputes it as police just harassing him.

Anyway, he's in jail.

"I know it's stressful." Malcolm says over the phone. "But hang in there. Everyone needs money."

"I know." Sean speaks into the receiver. "It's just I feel that this is all I'm going to do with my life, pushing carts and going nowhere."

"Well, you have other things. And it doesn't pay."

"Yeah." replies Malcolm. "There have been some strange things going on around town."

"Yes, I know." says Sean. "Animals and theft, it's amazing."

"I even heard squirrels are taking things from this jail. It's weird."

"Yeah and Bark O' Down wants Stopman to help him out." Sean scoffs. "He's so ridiculous."

Malcolm is at a phone in the Quad County slammer. "I know. You think Stops would take him up on that?"

"I don't think so, Mal." speaks Sean on the other line. *"Stopman doesn't take short-sighted profit for what he does."*

"I know. I hear he even drinks out of the Mayor's toilet." Malcolm says. "Bark, that is."

"Hey, I've got a job at the Quad City Country Club. You want to work there? It's temporary."

"Don't think so." Sean replies, while Carts stacked upon one another comes in a nearby bay. "My schedule's too unpredictable."

"Well, if you change your mind-"

"I already know it." says Sean. The young man hangs up, and gets back to work.

It's a crowded day at the *Stop Store,* and it is never a dull moment.

And it gets *very* interesting when a man in a tailor-made expensive suit, wearing a hound dog's mask approaches customer service.

The customers who see him muffle their snickers. The children they just outright laugh at him. This man in this mask is ignoring them. This man is the rich man, Bark O' Down.

"I sniffed and I *know* the Stopman is here." says the dog-masked man. Another man near him just guffaws with laughter, while others continue to watch.

"Sir, we don't know where Stopman would be." says the customer service lady, trying to hold back a smile.

"Look," barks Bark. "If you see him, tell him I'll give him what he wants."

He takes a paper and pin out of his suit pocket and writes out a figure.

"I'll offer him this much."
The lady customer service rep looks at the figure. She shakes her head. "I made more than that this morning."

While Bark O' Down is amusing people in that area of the store, a little girl is playing in the toy section. She sees a necklace.

All the while, a mysterious man from a darkened undisclosed location somehow communicates with a goose. Next to this man are a new car and that mountain of cash, stolen before.

The goose is on a pond next to the *Stop Store.* He files from there toward the building.

The girl grabs the necklace, which is on the floor.

Meanwhile, Bark continues to make offers (for Stopman) to the customer service cashier.

"I'll give him a spot on the game show 'You bet your bills." says the masked man. "He'll even get a shot at a new car."

"Will you be driving, dogface?" the lady asks.

As he continues his pleas, Bark continues to attract further attention. Even customers from the main cash registers are intrigued.

All the while, a lady grabs Sean next to a nearby plaza in the store.

"I can't find my little girl." she tells the cart pusher.

"I can take you to a manager." he says. "Come, let's go find one."

The goose under that man's control flies over the Stop Store. One of the solar domes that are built within the roof is under the bird.

The animal dives toward it.

"She's wearing a pink dress." the lady tells Sean. "I think she's in the toy section.

Still looking for a manager, Sean and the lady are near the toy section.

Then suddenly, that goose files through that dome. It takes everyone in the store by surprise.

The goose flies down to the sales floor. That girl grabs that necklace...and so does the goose. Both fly up toward the broken dome, and outside in the hot sunny day.

"My baby!" screams the girl's mother.

"Oh no!" exclaims Sean. He's looking like everyone else toward that broken dome. The goose and the girl are getting further and further away to the sky.

While everyone's attention is focused up, Sean slips out of people's sight, carefully during the pandemonium.

He heads to the restrooms nearby the toy section.

He enters the men's room quickly. He then stops short of the front entrance. He's see it *very* occupied. Men have even filled the stalls. He can't forget the smell either.

Sean covers his nose, and leaves the restroom.

Now, more people, including management gather beneath that open area in the roof. They are concerned.

The girl hangs on. The goose has the expensive necklace between his feet, as well as her.

Sean continues through the store. Then he runs through an aisle of the toy department. A red flash occurs in the middle of that aisle. No one, not even security guard and their cameras notice.

At the end of that aisle emerges STOPMAN!

The hero glows a bit. The kids are the first to notice him, then others. Some are skeptical.

"That's not Stopman." speaks one of the employees nearby. "It's just another lookalike."
Sean as Stopman then takes a hop. A red-beam under his feet pushes him toward that open roof and toward the sky with great speed.

He heads for that little girl.

"That…is…Stopman." says the corrected worker.

3

As the goose keeps flying, the girl continues to hang on. She looks down and then screams.

The flying goose then just notices her.

Turning his neck, he sees the child and hisses at her.

"Be nice." says the child to the goose.

Suddenly, a red-beam hits the bird. The girl let's go of the necklace.

"Ahh!" she screams.

Fortunately for her, she falls only a short distance, while the goose flies off. She is then immersed in red. The beam breaks her fall, leaving her prone in the sky albeit safe. The beam is connected and closes distance. On the other end is none other but the crimson and chrome crime-fighter, taking the child in his arms.

He holds her close and safe.

"Yay!" cheers the little girl.

"Take it easy, you're safe." assures Stopman.

"That was fun." she says. All the while, they both land on the Stop Store parking lot. Many people gather around; including Bark. He sifts his way through the crowd, next to the shiny crimson; who lands on his feet.

Stopman lays the child safe. Her mother takes her in her arms.

"Stopman, I want to offer you a great deal if you become my security." howls Bark O' Down.

"I don't guard pet food."
the hero insists.

"I'll give you just about
anything to stop my products
and pets from being stolen."
Barks says. "I'll even give you
discount on my dog biscuits.
They're delicious, I've tried
them."
"I don't own a dog." says
Stops.
"Well, neither do I." replies
Bark. "But I'm very rich. You own
a cat maybe?"

People with cameras gather
around the two. Blubs flash.

"I have so much invested in my pet shop empire." Bark continues. "Animals...my animals...even goldfish are escaping.

Stopman is agitated; not only by Bark but by those cameras. He feels the media potential for unkindness. He just wants to get away, especially from Bark.

He then points beyond the dog-masked rich man.

"Bark look," says the hero. "a fire hydrant!"

"Where?" Barks looks in the direction where the crimson hand has pointed. It gives the hero the opportunity to blast off in a red beam streak toward the sky.

Bark turns back around, and then looks up.

"Stopman!" yells Bark. "Call me, we'll have lunch!"

That goose now arrives over a golf-course with that necklace in his web-footed grasp. It is the Quad City Country Club, the largest in the city.

Honking from his mouth, he flies toward a golf hole on the green ground. As the flying fowl approaches it, the hole widens big enough for him to fit through. It widens to about three-feet in circumference; enough to allow the bird to fly through it.

Underneath this massive country club is where a Doctor Herman Vermain dwells. He has a unique ability to talk and control animals. He sits, as the goose comes to him from up above. In his hand he holds another necklace.

The goose lands at his feet.

"Honk! Honk! Honk!"
speaks the goose.

"Excellent James." speaks
the man known best as Dr. Ver-
Man. "I have such a selection of
jewelry, Sandris is bound to like
one of them."

"Honk! Honk!"

"Of course I won't
overwhelm her, I'll just turn on
the Vermain charm." he replies
to the goose.

Surrounding the doctor is
an abundance of stolen valuables.
From the car from that game-
show, to the money from the
bank, it blends in with the
assortment of animals.

It's almost like XANADU! In addition, an underground jungle is present. He is far enough below to not be noticed by the general public. Numerous animal sounds surround him. A black raven flies from one of the dark crevices of the cave-like atmosphere.

The goose drops the necklace before him. He stands and picks it up.

"Whatever issue people have with me, I will rise." insists the doctor, dress in a dirty trench coat and a mousse-laden Mohawk.

"For a long time I had neither the money, and I guess neither the class to be among certain people." he continues. "But now, there's nothing that will come between me and my love."

The goose honks his attention.

" 'Just be myself'?" Ver-Man responds. "That's not what works here."

"Honk! Honk!"

"Well of course I'd be surprised." replies the Doctor. "Not as surprised as when those people would see me again."

The goose honks some more.

The raven calls out.

"Look it, I'm not going to sit and listen to this debate." he says.

His picture of Seandris is enshrined right next to him.

"Soon, I will leave her breathless, mostly." guarantees De. Ver-Man. "You'll see, goose."

"Honk."

" 'Not my crowd'? Don't you see, places like this is supposed to be where prosperity lay."

"Honk. Honk. Honkity, Honk!"

" 'Laugh at me.'?" the Doctor repeats. "not with all of this, and the car; and the suit too."

Dr. Ver-Man points to all of the stolen valuables. "Thanks to my animal brethren, I now feel I have everything I need. Now she has to take notice."

4

It's corporate visiting day at the Stop-Store.

Sean leaves from the personnel office located in the back of the store. He had tried to ask the store manager for work, but he is too preoccupied.

"How did a priceless necklace get out of the jewelry-counter and into the toy department?" asks a scolding corporate executive.

"Don't know, sir." says the store's top man. "Maybe a mouse tried to lift it...before the bird, that is."

As the manager gets
scolded further Sean takes out
his cellphone. He dials a number.

"Hello." says Malcolm on the
other end.

"Mal." says Sean. He is next
to the barber shop. "It's me."

"Are you alright?"

Yeah, I just want to know if that
country club job is still open?"

"Well, I can check." speaks
Malcolm from his cell.

"With the club having a reputation for being haunted, I'm sure I can get you in."

"Haunted?" inquires Sean.

"Yeah, in addition to stuff being stolen, people hear and see strange stuff around the mansion and the rest of the property." says Malcolm. "There have been reports of ghosts floating objects, and even the eyes of paintings moving."

"Well, there's always a cure for the boogey man." speaks Sean on Malcolm's opposite line.

You can just hear the sound of jail in Malcolm's background; cells slamming shut, keys jangling and what not.

"I'll check it out," says Malcolm. "In the meantime, keep your head up. You're a good man in spite of it all."

"There are always alternatives."

"Thanks, man." speaks Sean. He disconnects.

Walking over to the electronics part of the store, he sees his girlfriend Natalie.

QCBC news is on. Sean joins her in watching.

"Bark O' Down has made another offer to the Unstoppable Stopman." speaks the pretty woman on-screen.

"Apparently, the masked dog has asked to relay that he wants the crimson and chrome crime-fighter to guard the armored car, that'll help escort the money for the tycoon's upcoming charity event benefitting...orphaned animals."

"Hmm..." says Natalie. "Stopman's integrity is on the line.

"You think so, huh?" Sean asks the woman.

"Yes." she replies. "I wonder if Stops would say no to a charity."

Sean kisses her and they continue walking around the area. He has a lot on his mind. Sometimes the stress makes him wish he was elsewhere.

And, speaking of elsewhere...

Dr. Ver-Man watches that same news broadcast, behind that underground jungle full of life. I mean, you can hear it.

The Doctor watches the program and smiles. With the raven on his coated shoulder, he looks at the armored truck, upon a stolen wide-screen television.

In the trees of the jungle behind him is a massive figure, which is silhouetted in the background. It is Simian-like in its form.

The Doctor is up to something.

At QCBC studios on the Quad City strip there's a lot going on. In the main studio, Bark's pet telethon is being set up. And no one else, than the dog-masked wonder is giving orders.

"More stuffed animals on that side." Commands Bark, who's working with the technical crew onstage.

The set has an array of devices resembling a telethon studio. It has a number of telephones, a panel of desks and too, stuffed animals all over. Various people all around Bark prepare for this function.

With people everywhere around Bark, he barely notices the presence of one chrome-laden crime-fighter; that is until he looks in that direction.

The crimson shine of Stopman himself is due in part to the studio lights reflecting the redness of his suit. Stop's appearance is gaudy in audition, no doubt.

Bark is unimpressed.

"Bark Down?" says the hero.

The canine-faced man sighs. "Look, I've enough look-alikes already." he insists. "Go away."

He turns from Stopman.

That's when the hero fires an octagon-shaped beam all over Bark O' Down.

Dogface can't move. He is prone in his stance. He can only breathe.

The other people around him notice, and are stunned.

Stopman walks around to face him in the center of the studio.

"That's just to prove I am who you've been asking about." says Stopman.

Bark's eyes move, but he is still motionless.

"Don't worry Mr. Down." he continues. "My pause beam is only temporary. I better speak before, your security comes."

He begins right away.

"So, since this is for charity, I want to deal."

The hero looks around for a moment. He then continues.

"I've thought about your proposition. I've decided to guard that charity. However, I want compensation of my own."

One of Bark's assistants sees the scenario from the bleachers. He goes to possibly get security.

"I will guard your interest, if you agree to a price." he continues. "And have my comp. sent to a P.O. box."

As more people gather around the stage, Stopman pulls a sheet of paper from his crimson tights.

Bark then snaps out of the pause-beam.

"Whoa!" barks Bark. He shakes his head; then looks to Stopman.

"It's really you?" smiles the man in the dog mask.

He hands him the paper. Bark snatches it after a momentary reluctance. He reads that paper.

The masked man scoffs. "That's more than my dog biscuits."

"Take it or leave it." speaks Stops, while security is sifting through the crowd. "Comic book heroes usually do not perform these kind of negotiations, but this is not a comic book."*

*
;)

Bark takes one look at him.

Here comes the rent-a-cops on the set. They are still at least thirty-feet away the pair, and still within the crowd.

"Okay...fine." Bark agrees. "Just you know, that failure to guard my interest will result in consequence, I don't care how powerful you are."

"Fine." agrees Stopman.

The guards with Bark's assistant arrive; yet Stopman runs into the nearest crowd, gone.

The assistant stands next to O' Down. They look in the direction where the crimson-coated man has departed.

"Do you think he knows about—"

"No." Bark cuts in. "Keep silent about that."

The man looks around the stage.

"Besides, it's SHOWTIME!" yells Bark. His voice echoes through the studio. "I need a drink, where a fire hydrant?"

5

LIGHTS!

CAMERA!

ACTION!

"Live from Quad City, U.S.A. strip, the entertainment mecca...for tonight, it's the BARK'S PETS TELETHON!" speaks an announcer to the viewers, like yourself. If one's watching on television, they see the spectacle that make the city's best strip one of the most visually interesting in the world.

"Hosted by Bark O' Down:
owner & entrepreneur."

The screens all over shows
Bark with a glass of Champaign.
He laps his tongue inside the
glass. The announcer continues.

"Coming up...Bark's mongrel
orchestra...and
featuring...the poodle-faced
dancers!"

The images show
themselves respectively, with
each name announced.

"also-entertaining reading from...Jesse Mathes!" ☺

"And now people...here's..." right after the announcer speaks occurs a barking sound effect. The audience waits, while Bark emerges from the curtain in a tux.

The applause comes. Bark greets the audience. Too bad some of them were paid to be present.

"Thanks one and all." He speaks.

"I want to thank those who have made the donations, but we must have more to fight this here...pet shop disease that-"

His assistant director off-camera immediately whispers toward him. Bark lifts his hound ear to listen.

"What?"

The audience stands by, as the dog-masked man hears the loud whisper.

"Oh..." Bark says aloud. He's now embarrassed.

"I...mean...orphaned pets...and such."

The audience is silent. He sweats under that canine mask. Looking at the camera, he takes a breath, rubbing the back of his neck.

"Uh...let's take another look at the total, while my mongrel orchestra plays."

The total board is without numbers; the dog-mask band nearby plays to a building crescendo. The numbers begins to form.

"Here it comes." says Bark.

Meanwhile, at a couple of blocks down from the studio, a "panhandler" sits in the city night with a table next to him. The table is covered halfway with a sheet. A streetlight is the only presence; amongst his very own.

Then, a man in a suit and trench-coat approaches him.

"Can you spare some change?" says the borrower to the well-dressed man.

"But of course." replies the dapper-looking man, who puts his briefcase on that table.

As the man searches his trench-coat for "change", the table rotates. A duplicate of that *same* briefcase is in its place.

Almost unnoticed was the subtle way in which that "panhandler" rotated it. He just pressed a button behind that furniture.

Anyhow, the man gives him a thousand-dollar-bill; then grabs that switched case.

All the while from a nearby tall building is that simian figure, once present in Ver-Man's underground. The figure witnesses the exchange.

At the same time, Stopman, the armored truck, and its guards are at the backdoor entrance of that studio. The truck's backdoor's are open. Present inside are only a few envelopes. There seems to be no tidy sum.

Stops is currently in an uncomfortable position. Not only does he have the job at hand on his mind, but paparazzi are there flashing pictures of the hero. Guards do their best to brush the photographers away. Then Bark's assistant arrives out of the studio back door, next to him.

"So, where's the money?" Stopman asks.

The assistant produces a smile. "Well, I'm embarrassed. We've tallied the amounts before the public...uh...these are just checks from earlier. More's to come."

That panhandler arrives at the truck. This time he is wearing a security-guard suit. He has that briefcase, which was switched.
Stopman observes it, only not too closely. The man puts that briefcase in the back of the armored vehicle. Two guards go in.

"We're ready to go." says Bark's assistant. Cameras still flash. Stopman cannot wait to leave the area. The assistant looks to him.

"Bark would like for you to stand on top of the truck." he tells the crimson hero.

Stopman is puzzled. Then, comes a helicopter above them all. A light from it flashes down at them.

"Are you serious?" speaks Stops.

The assistant gives him a stern look. "Look, we're paying you a handsome figure chrome-dome." insults the assistant. "It's also show-business. WE need you to give a publicity boost to Bark and his company."

"But, I am here to guard your interest."

"Yes, but things could go bad if you are uncooperative in any way."

Stopman bites his lip. Reluctantly, he accepts the flakiness of the situation, and climbs the truck.

The guards beneath him
close the truck. Stopman asks no
questions...right now. Yet, he is
suspicious. Yet, there he is
playing ball and balancing himself
atop an armored truck.

Then, the vehicle moves. Stops
loses balance for a moment.

"To International Square!" yells
the assistant. It takes off, and
Stopman regains his balance
atop it.

That simian figure is atop
another building. As the truck
moves, he hops across the
different buildings following.

Stopman rides atop, feeling like an ornament. The truck goes through the city and the helicopter above is following with the spotlight. People are even along the road, either cheering or heckling, taking pictures or videos, or both.

Stopman feels so exploited. He doesn't feel it's worth the trouble. But he's a man of his word. He'll just be glad when it'll be over; especially with Bark's likeness on either side of the armored truck.

And speaking of...

6

"Now people, those tallies are pitiful." says Bark to the audience watching at home and in person.

The numbers are already hidden.

"We need more so these animals can receive the care they so well deserve."

He doesn't tell people that maybe most of those donations will not go to the charity he has named.

He then lifts his doggie ear to listen in on his microphone.

"Wait..." he says aloud, center stage. He continues to listen.

Then, he smiles.

"We are going live to an armored truck, that carries a great amount of our donations."

A screen on the stage lowers from the ceiling. All the while, phone operators are standing by on that stage, bored to death.

No phones are ringing at this point, which could be detrimental to the ratings.

When that screen finishes
lowering, the image on it
projects that armored truck
driving across the city via a
camera from that helicopter. It
still has the spotlight on it.

Stopman stands on top of it in
the center.

"Those current donations
are now being escorted to a
secure area." says Bark. "We of
my conglomerates take our
security seriously."

From the helicopter, the camera
zooms in on Stops.

"We have hired the Unstoppable Stopman, who sponsors this charity. And *he* supports me and my philanthropy."

He motions to the screen. The image of the truck and Stopman is shown by the millions at home. All the while, the truck eventually stops at an intersection's stoplights after coming off a highway. International Square Mall is just around the corner.

"So, while that's happening, I now present the Poodle-faced dancers!" announces Bark.

The audience applauds, while women with literally poodle masks on their faces begin a chorus line, as the band plays on. People watching at home see a split-screen of the dog-faced dancers on one side, and the truck and Stopman on another.

Stopman, the driver, and two guards placed inside the back wait for the stoplight to change.

Then...from up above a nearby building...comes that simian figure.

The now identified ape emerges among the streetlights, the helicopter spotlight, and on top of Stopman.

The armored truck bends from that simian's weight. The backdoor of the vehicle is forced wide-open. The whole truck is now prone and broken.

Andy the Ape beats his chest on top of Stopman's chest.

Everyone watches it sees it on T.V., including Dr. Ver-Man from his underground. He laughs.

The crimson-chrome crime-fighter is disoriented. The red glow of his body flickers on and off.

Andy Ape is one of Dr. Ver-Man's most trusted animals. He is about a half of ton in weight; very big, and no doubt powerful. One of the security guards comes out of the back. He tries to raise his rifle.

Andy Ape is close enough to smack that guard aside and very far away into the night. The driver and that other guard is unconscious inside.

With his hand, Andy Ape rips open a piece of that back truck. He comes off of Stopman, who gathers himself. The ape then grabs that briefcase. He begins to walk down the open street. Very few cars are around. Those who *are* around are stunned.

Then, Stopman stands.

"Hold it!" insists the crime fighter.

"Don't do it." whispers Ver-Man, from his perch at his location. "Just walk away."

Andy Ape stops in his tracks. His back is turned from Stops. He drops the case, turning around to face the chrome hero.

Stopman glows again.

More people all around begin to gather in the city night.

The simian charges the Stopman. His momentum catapults the red hero about 200 meters down the road.

The ape turns and grabs that case again. He hops off the smashed armored truck.

Immediately, a glow of red comes charging back toward the animal from 200 meters. Before Stopman can connect, the ape moves sideways instinctively. He grabs the glowing hero's open right Achilles area. It jolts Stops suddenly.

The ape swings him a couple of times.

He tosses Stopman again, this time further down the street; perhaps in another borough of the city.

Then, Andy Ape with the case still in hand, hops away to the opposite direction. He hops over and over again into the darkness of the night across Quad City U.S.A.

While all of this occurs, it is being recorded via the camera in that helicopter. The whole world watches. Most are captivated.

Phones at the telethon start ringing some more.

At one of the movie theaters in the city, the audience there is watching the horror movie "Your Mummy's ugly in 3-D" a man eating nachos is about to watch a pivotal scene within the film.

Then Stopman crashes through the screen.

He lands on that movie goer. Nachos and cheese smother the man's new shirt. Everyone else in the theater scream and scatter.

"Blast it!" yells the smothered man. "This is my new shirt!"

It's a mix of confusion, chaos and applause. It seemed to the movie goers that the film had come to life. Well, most have their 3-D glasses on. It's such an impact.

It doesn't help by now that Stops is covered in wraps and popcorn. He scares the audience. He has some resemblance of the main character on that movie screen.

7

A short time later, Stops returns to the scene of the crime. All is left is the wrecked truck and other things suggesting the presence of a beast.

Next to the rubble of the vehicle is where Stopman stands. More people are now present. They see him. Jeers start to grow around him. Others just watch. Stops is taken aback. Well, the bright side is that he's not hit with a rotten tomato.

SPLAT!!!!!!

Oops...spoke too soon.

The crime-fighter just coolly observes, among other things, the heavy simian footprints imbedded in the city streets. At the same time, the police, fire and ambulance services tend to the other pieces of mayhem now present after the melee.

They work around Stopman. He flies off.

Later on that night, a dead end is where Sean Paus ends up. He had tracked those final gorilla prints laid behind the Dead End sign before him. In addition, there are lots of trees behind the sign.

And behind those countless trees hidden somewhat is the Quad City Country Club among other places.

Sean is puzzled. He can't see a way where the ape has disappeared. However, with that country club straight ahead, and a specific clue, he won't stop his curious search. One way or another he wants to get to the bottom of this whole thing. He cannot find Andy Ape, yet a clue keeps Sean alert.

The clue is that he smells animals. And the smell is very conspicuous.

Sean walks away into the night along a darkened street. Although he's not one clue as to where that ape may have gone, the simian is close by, but hidden.

Right under the nose of the man who is Stopman, is that massive underground lair with Dr. Ver-Man at the head. It stretches vastly and inconspicuously across the underbelly of that country club and other properties. Many passages hidden and otherwise are present. It is like a complex maze that only an expert could master.

Andy Ape comes out of that underground jungle, delivering that briefcase to the doctor at his perch. The doctor grabs it. Opening it before the simian, it is revealed that the case is filled with Quad City bearer bonds, which can give him all the gold in the world...if he wants.

"Excellent." speaks Ver-Man. "Now, I've got full financial clout. Seandris will have to *definitely* fawn over my pull. Now, being poor won't be an excuse.

The doctor seems to have everything he wants. The raven on his shoulder caws and flaps his wings.

Before the other animals, the doctor sighs and thinks. "When I was in high school they teased, Herman Vermain." he says. "They used to say 'Herman Vermin', 'Herman Vermin'."

The animals continue listening.

"Now, at that Country Club ball coming soon, I can come out of that sick conformed shell that those in sick society seemed to put me in. It will be the perfect time to impress Seandris. Oh, my love she will be.

He looks to her picture next to him. "Then, all of those snobs shall eat crow."

The raven flaps and caws on the doctor's shoulder.

"It's just a figure of speech." Ver-Man tells the raven.

Animals come and go in this underbelly location. It's a casual area for most non-humans. Among the other animals in that special audience is the goose, who cries out toward the odd doctor.

"I *will* be myself." the doctor tells the goose. "It'll be fine."

"Honkity! Honk."

"No, I don't underestimate their cruelty." he says. "I'm there for *her* not them. And wait until they see my suit...Rather wait until *she* sees my suit."

"Honk! Honk!"

"You watch your language." Ver-Man tells the long-neck bird. "I'm going to be the big talk of that party above ground."

The Quad City Chronicle the next day prints a headline:

"LOCAL DOG-FACED TYCOON SUES STOPMAN"

Sean this next morning is at his home. He's watching the news.

"Oh brother." Sean states to himself. Watching the media with Natalie, he just wants to regurgitate; not unusual, considering the media's sickness...sometimes.

The lady on Sean's television reports the topic:

Bark O' Down claims that Stopman had failed to live up to his bargain of being an effective bodyguard for the tycoon's interest." she speaks to the public. *"even if none of the charity money had been stolen."*

Sean scoffs.

"When asked about the valuable stolen bonds recently," says the news reporter. *"Bark barked 'no comment', thus continuing his harangue against Stopman."*

Sean just shakes his head, staring contemptuously at the screen.

"Dogface even took his account from the Stop Store." Natalie tells Sean, while leaning her head on his shoulder. Both are sitting on a couch.

"Yeah." Sean responds. "I tried to get some hours today." he looks at her. "Manager says that they'll have to lay-off more people. And I'm broke, although I feel I'm owed."

Natalie stands from the couch. "Better find work." Natalie says. "Bills cost money."

She leaves his home. Afterwards, Sean gets on his stationary phone.

"Bearer bonds?" Sean whispers to himself out of curiosity. The phone rings on the other side.

Someone picks up on the opposite end of the line.

"Hello." speaks Malcolm.

"Stopman got screwed." Sean tells his friend.

"I know." Malcolm replies. "I was thinking that if a position is open for that country club gig, I'd like to fill it. I need the money."

"Bark never paid Stops, huh?"

"Not a cent." Sean speaks into the receiver. "It's all over the news."

A co-exist banner covers the underground jungle behind Dr. Ver-Man. He stands before his many different animals.

"My friends," begins the doctor. "We've come a long way."

Animal sounds emanate across the underground.
        "Many great people want to invoke change. I'm one of them."

He paces across his perch.

        "It would seem that intolerance and indifference is rotting away the fabrics that matter to most of us. It's always seen on T.V."

He stops pacing. He looks out to that audience of animals.

"But I want to prove that
this is the U.S.A. and all, or most
has the capacity to overcome
the negative." he speaks with his
tone rising.
   "I want more than to win the
affection of this woman." he
continues, looking at her picture
nearby.
   "I want to win the integrity of
those who are privileged to be
more fortunate than most."

With the raven still on his
shoulder, he raises his arms.

"I've often thought that the rich could be nicer people." he states. "I think they could, if others, like me make the right impression."

But what is the right impression within that context? Does the doctor even know?

Anyway, all the animals, especially the raven responds positively; with exception the goose, who is front and center. The bird hangs his head low. The body language of the goose is negative. The doctor pays no attention. He adjourns to a nearby dressing room.

Inside that dressing room he grabs the suit he will wear at that banquet. It is wrapped in black plastic protectant. He looks to it.

"Look out Seandris," he states. "Here come the doctor, and his truest self."

8

It's Friday in Quad City U.S.A. At the Quad City Country Club this day is a festive one. The sun's just now setting upon this gala spectacle. It is now a hot summer night. The moon's full, and already present, before the sun leaves the sky. This country club glows within the Quad City, U.S.A. area.

Much of Quad City's richest and most affluent are attending the location. It is very much a gaudy scene. Lights and jewelry sparkle; especially among one of the handful of the country club's castles among the property; the main castle.

Those who are employed there are a mix of veteran workers and temporary workers. The workers could do fine work, even with pressure from their bosses.

Sean and Malcolm meet their immediate boss, Swilly Green; who's in charge of assigning them their positions. The three men are at an isolated part of the castle's kitchen.

"Malcolm you'll serve for tonight." Swilly tells Malcolm. "And Sean, well you might have to do some night caddying."

"Night caddying, sir?" Sean asks.

"Yes, Howard Preppie is one of our finest members." says Swilly. "He likes to get in a game, sometimes during these get-togethers."

"What about this place being haunted?" Malcolm asks straight up.

Swilly is silent. He takes a deep breath and then answers.

"We don't really talk about that." admits their boss. "But I can say that no one's found 'Herman Vermin' yet."

"Who's that?" Sean asks.

"Herman Vermin worked here some time ago." says Swilly.

"He was so unpopular that Howard's son, Paul Preppie played a cruel joke on him."

Sean and Malcolm look at each other, and then back to Swilly.

"I won't get into detail about how the joke was played." Swilly admits. "But, let's just say that it ended up with Herman being exposed to radiation."

"Really?" asks Malcolm.

"For all anyone knows, he was last seen rushing to a shower and then he disappeared." Swilly continues.

"Since he's been gone, strange occurrences have been happening all over the property. And it's been hard sometimes hiring people."

"Don't worry," Sean tells Swilly. "We'll do our best."
"Good." Swilly says. "Meantime, ask around if you need help."
Swilly walks away. Malcolm turns to Sean. "I guess I'll get ready."
"Me too." Sean says.
Malcolm grabs a server uniform, while Sean exits to the outside.

On the moonlit lawn of the golf course, Sean walks across it. He's impressed by the scenery, but in an investigative mood.

"Hey, boy?" says a man's voice next to a golf tee.

Sean looks, and sees an older man in very awful golf pants. The man is Howard Preppie. He's there with at least three other men; all of whom are his entourage. Sean approaches them.

"Carry my bags, let's be snappy." Howard orders.

Sean obliges. The men gather in the golf cart, and take off. While Sean walks, with a heavy golf bag. That golf cart is speeding on.

"Hurry up Caddy!" yells Howard Preppie. "I want to get in 18 holes for the night!"

After some time, people are eating and dancing in and around the greens. However, hidden somewhat are the many animals that are present. They harbor many different hiding places.

Spencer the dog has a hidden spot near the dining area. Although it is crowded, the dog manages to hide under a white-clothed table.

The canine sees and smells a steak.

He licks his chops.

Speaking of the doctor's animals, a lot of them hide and peek through holes and other hiding places throughout this posh mansion.
As people carry on festively, eyes on a painting of a historic figure, hung up above a living room full of dancing guest begins to move.

Behind it and the walls is actually Dr. Ver-Man, checking out the scene.

"Excellent." speaks the doctor hidden in this passage. "The party's going well."

Most don't notice the eyes move on this painting of Snorky Wagner, the first settler of Quad City. Yet, a lady server does. She seems very much a jumpy type. Watching those eyes move, she shakes with fear. Holding a tray full of glasses of Champaign, she drops it. Then, she runs to the kitchen as quick as she can.

All the while, the guest eating are living and laughing it up; especially at that table with a steak.

The man eating the steak is only started to cut it. He communicates with the other people at that table.

"It's not a mere coincidence that rich people are smarter than poor people. We pay more for education." says the man. Everyone hangs on his word. "Instead of telling those with no money to get a job, I tell them to buy a lottery ticket."

The guests laugh.

Yet, no one including this man does not notice Spencer's paw reach and grab this man's steak. Only the vegetables are left.

"Yes, let the poor eat hamburger steak." speaks the rich man. "We always have the choice cut."

He goes to cut his steak. Then, he and the others at the table notice his steak is gone. The man's eyes widen.

"Waiter!" yells the man.

"I'm telling you I'm quitting." says the lady who saw those eyes move. "This place is haunted, and I know it!"

Malcolm is there with this lady. They are in the kitchen again. It is busy and rustling. "It's probably just your imagination."

Meanwhile, one of the chef's prepares desert for the guests. In a hidden slot within the kitchen, a bumble bee looks to the honey on the table. This insect goes back into the hidden area of this slot, and "tells" his follow bees. In an instant, the swarm of bees enters a plastic bag with a sophisticated device which inflates instantly, once the bees fill it up. Within it, the electrical device serves as an engine.

One of the bees drives it. It floats and flies. These are smart animals.

At another hidden passage among the mansion walls, Andy Ape is eyeing bananas on the desert buffet table.

Yes, these are also hungry animals.

Even the raven spots a big plate of escargot. By coincidence, it is Malcolm's serving tray, in which this dish is located. He then carries the tray over his right shoulder. Unbeknownst to him, or even the guests, the raven gets under a nearby white table cloth. He flies, and lands upon the escargot, and starts to eat the snails. The tray is covered by the cloth.

After flying off, Malcolm still doesn't notice, but that plate is a mess, with no snails.

Arriving at the table he's supposed to serve the dish, Malcolm lays the tray down. The lady who ordered the escargot isn't amused.

"Hey, what are you trying to pull?" she complains.

Malcolm then notices the plate, and is perplexed.

"What?" chides the lady. "Did a ghost take my food?"

Malcolm blinks. He shakes his head incredulously at the wrecked plate.

Another member of the country club is Paul Preppie the son of Howard. He's had too much to drink. In his drunken stupor, he approaches the band.

"Hey!" says the band leader, as Paul grabs the microphone. Eventually…he howls into the microphone. Everyone notices. He has a familiarity about him, but more or that eventually.

"Give me a wedge." orders Howard Preppie on the green.

Not knowing what a wedge is in golf terms, Sean grabs a putter.

"No. No!" says Howard. "I said a wedge!"

Howard pushes Sean out of the way. He grabs the golf club he wants. As he does, Sean notices a dog mask at the bottom of the case carrying the elder Preppie's clubs.

Sean notices it for a moment. It looks like the "face" of Bark O' Down. Immediately, his anger and suspicions arise. His anger arises, because Bark never paid him for Stopman's services. He's suspicious, because of the mask obviously.

"I'll remember this, come tip time." speaks Howard.

Is he *this* man? Sean wonders in his mind, as Howard swings at the ball.

He immediately slices into the nearest trees.

Sean rolls his eyes, trying to focus on his job. "This is going to be a long night, I bet."

Still on the stage, Paul Preppie takes a drink of a glass of Champaign in hand. The members who know Paul are embarrassed. He continues to howl.

The workers are laughing, along with some of the guests. However, more antics are yet to come.

In a dark and abandoned dining room, that scared maid is frozen again. The tray she holds is shaking.

A jar of honey is "floating" across the darkened area. She thinks she sees an unexplained monstrous blob above it. She also hears what she perceives as a ghost humming. It's actually the bees in that bag.

Anyway, it scares her. She drops her tray, and runs back to the kitchen.

Confusion is starting to rock the mansion. At the entrance arrives another car. It's the one from that game show.

9

The car's driver's door opens up. Who comes out of it perplexes the valet.

Out comes a chimpanzee in a chauffer's suit and hat. The valet is stunned even further when the monkey gives the man a tip...a bunch of bananas.

And speaking of bananas...

Paul Preppie has stopped singing, and has decided to mingle at the buffet table. Next to him, next to the bananas especially is Andy Ape...in disguise.

The Ape wears a
Halloween mask of a blond-
haired, man. The simian's
massive bulk is covered in beige
of a stretched trench-coat.

Andy tries stuffing himself,
by lifting that mask as subtly as
he can, and eating those bananas.

Paul Preppie rudely taps him
on the shoulder.

"Great party, isn't it?" slurs
Paul Preppie with a smile.

As the drunken man
staggers, Andy tries ignoring
him with just a grunt, and his
back turned.

Paul makes a fool of himself.

He is about to make an even bigger fool of himself. That lady, Seandris arrives at this table next to him. She looks classy-perfect, with a glass of Champaign in her hand.

"Hey darling." belches Paul. "I'm a rich, sexy, single man. Let's get out of here and ride off in the moonlit night."

Seandris is taken aback by his curtness.

Paul smiles to her face.

Seandris frowns; then throws that glass of Champaign in his face.

That chauffer (chimpanzee) opens the passenger door. Dr. Ver-Man gets out that car. The valets all around the door of the mansion drop their collective jaws.

"But I really saw it!" the maid tells Malcolm.

"This *is* a strange place." adds Malcolm. The two are in one of the worker's lounge. Malcolm looks around. Then, he hears a squeak, and sees something which holds his attention.

A squirrel (yes, a squirrel) is pulling walnuts in a bowl, on the floor toward a dark corridor ahead.

"Hmm," says Malcolm watching that squirrel. "I've heard this place has hidden parts."

The maid is sitting in a chair. She's too freaked out to notice those nuts and the critter.

The dish from the dishwasher, huh?" asks the maid.

"No." says Malcolm. "just from the boss, maybe."

In the darkness of the corridor before the ballroom, Dr. Ver-Man walks alone. He's moments away from being exposed to this particular public.

"For the last time, and for *years*, the answer is no!" Seandris tells Paul, who still presses.

"Aw, come on!" says the drunkard. "I'm rich. That's all a woman needs, when it comes to me!"

Suddenly, Paul grabs his stomach. Then he walks over to the bar.

Instead of ordering a drink, he goes belly-over the bar-table and retches like crazy. The whole ballroom hears him throw up.

"Typical." says the lady, not surprised.

While Paul Preppie is doing what he's doing, and the doctor is approaching the public, Howard Preppie is continuing his golf game. It's about the 3rd hole. He's out of the trees, but he cheated his way to the open green.

Once again the elder Preppie swings his club. This time, the ball lands within the course's deep wishing well.

Howard and his entourage all look to Sean.

"Are you kidding?" he tells them.

"Go retrieve the ball, or you're fired!" insists the pushy rich man.

Sean sighs, and then scoffs. He reluctantly approaches that wishing well. He knows that he couldn't reach that far down; that is, not as Sean Paus.

Deep in that well, the goose, Jim had been hit with that golf ball. Sean approaches that old well. He goes to stare down into it.

Suddenly, the golf ball flies back out of the well. How it flew back up that far and such is a mystery to Sean.

The ball is back on the green. Yet, Sean stares with great curiosity in that dark well.

"Hurry, boy!" yells an impetuous Howard. "Are you making a wish?"

Sean turns slowly around from the well. "You have no idea." he says to himself.

Howard swings again.

The ball lands in another set of trees.

Sean sees that ball disappears again. That castle of a mansion is upon the long background, on a hill. The moon shines still.

Sean, without looking toward Howard goes to those trees.

Seandris looks board, after witnessing Paul doing his retching.

Then, she looks to the entrance of the ballroom.

What she now sees piques her interest.

"What the?" replies the rich beauty with her mouth wide open.

The others in the ballroom follow suit. Even the band is silent.

Paul then finally rises up from over that bar table. At first, he doesn't look in that direction. Then, he does stare that way, after noticing everyone looking too.

Malcolm follows that squirrel into another dark corridor. The maid follows him. She is frantic. A stiff breeze would scare her.

Then, the two look ahead of them. They see what appears to be a ghost.

It's that cloth worn by that raven. It flies towards them. The maid is shaken further.

"I'm getting the heck out of here." she screams in panic.

The lady runs the opposite direction. Malcolm though is unafraid, and just moves out of the raven's way.

He doesn't buy the ghost theory. With the maid gone, he decides to follow the flying sheet. The raven is going where the squirrel had gone on the ground.

"I don't believe it." Seandris whispers aloud. "You can't be serious."

Paul's eyes widen. Andy Ape is still next to him.

Under his mask, the simian is the only one appreciating the presence of one Dr. Ver-Man.

Now, all eyes are on Dr. Ver-Man and his "gala" attire.

"Hurry up, Caddy!" yells Howard Preppie beyond the trees, where Sean is concealed.

"A needle in a haystack." Sean laments to himself. He's now buried in the trees around him.

With the moon shining, Sean discovers a golf ball. In fact, there are countless golf balls within a stream running into a pond, further down the course.

Sean doesn't care. He just grabs one, and throws it out toward the open green.

Suddenly, just as soon as he had thrown out that ball, Howard throws it back. It hits Sean in the forehead, which causes a small red flash upon his head.

"Negative, that's not the one." yells Howard on the outside of those trees. "It's a Q.C.C.C. Prestige.

Sean bites his lip. He just cannot believe he's searching for a special golf ball in the dark.

10

The silence is so in the ballroom, that crickets seem to chirp.

Finally, the silence is broken by Paul.

He laughs loudly.

"Look everybody, it's Herman Vermin!"

The rest of the room just hears Paul's loud guffaw. That laughs registers a big negative in the doctor's psyche. It doesn't help that his black and white plaid suit doesn't register with these social prestige types either.

Speaking of, let's talk of his wardrobe for a moment, and while Paul continues his drunken laughter.

The moon in a giant window close by shines on honestly...a bad fashion tip. That is, at least how most of these club members see it.

Only the drunkard Paul Preppie reacts most visibly; some have muffled snickers. Most are shocked, because many didn't realize that he was alive.

Undaunted, he tries ignoring the Preppie named Paul. With an inept choice for a suit, he approaches Seandris.

"Hello." says the doctor to her, in his friendliest tone. The moon shines on her beauty, as well. His greeting to her is for the world to see.

Then, she reacts.

"You're weird." Seandris tells the doctor coldly, and with her nose turned upward to the moon.

Paul laughs even harder.

Dr. Ver-Man is shocked. His mind begins to race; then further emotional pain.

"Looking like garbage as usual, Vermin!" says Paul.

Preppie tries getting closer to the doc, stumbling.

Then, Andy Ape in disguise hops in front of Dr. Ver-Man. The simian faces Paul.

The Ape smacks Mr. Preppie *hard.*

Somehow, Paul flies out of that giant window. He crashes out of it.

Dr. Ver-Man is frozen and hurt. Seandris tries to give distance by slowly moving away from Ver-Man and the masked ape.

From his point of view, Sean sees Paul's body flying across the green and into some more trees.

"Chop! Chop!" says Howard. "Or else."

Sean ignores Howard's voice. He sees his golf ball, though. Yet, his attention fixes on the palace on the hill.

Seandris is taken aback.

Then, the laughter from the club members come; though they do not laugh at the doctor, per se. However, as the laughter grows, Ver-Man begins to notice them.

He thinks within his emotionally shattered state that everybody's laughing at him.

Seandris begins to disappear in the crowd.

Outside, an assortment of animals begin rising from out of the ground. The many secret passages across the massive land begin to be exposed, and Sean witnesses it.

"Disperse." Dr. Ver-Man speaks to the crowd.

They laugh even louder. The doctor sheds a shameful tear.

"What a celebration!" speaks one of the laughing snobs.

"Everyone DISPERSE!" yells the doctor.

"No!" exclaims the unmoving crowd.

Wild animals are filling up the golf course. They begin to wreck the scene.

Sean can't take it anymore.

"Remind me to fire this caddy." Howard tells another partner on that hole.

"If he hasn't found my ball by now-"

A golf ball then hits Howard Preppie *hard* in his face. It surprises his entourage.

Stopman then flies out of those trees, and then toward the party palace.

The crowds of club members focus on the unmoving Dr. Ver-Man. Andy Ape stands there too.

He hears phrases in his mind:

"Herman Vermin! Hermin Vermin!"

"Looking like garbage as usual, Vermin."

"You're weird!"

"Honk. Honk. Honkity! Honk!"

Dr. Ver-Man summons another animal, while the other animals emerge right outside. Andy Ape keeps on his mask, and roars. The snobs are unmoved.

They laugh further, unafraid of the simian. The ape goes into the crowd, right after Seandris, with mask still on.

At the same time, a skunk emerges from out of nowhere; front and center before the crowd.

Immediately, they all scream and disperse in chaos. Most begin to head outside in the hot night.

The chauffer (chimpanzee) helps himself to the bananas at the fruit buffet.

Andy Ape grabs Seandris.

She screams.

The melee emerges outside. It's like a zoo of loose animals. Many of these people are in danger. Panic is spread wide.

A rhino comes charging at a couple near the sands, head-on. The animal comes even closer.

Then, the Stopman comes in-between the couple and that rhinoceros.

A big red-beamed octagon-shaped shield comes up before the animal, and he slams into it. Stopman's feet and calves bury in the white grains. That couple he has saved just backs away, witnessing.

"Bravo." claps the man of the couple; so inept an attitude.

The rhino lays there unconscious.

Stopman looks to the couple, who just gets a flippant kick out of what they've just seen.

"Get somewhere safe!" Stops insists to that couple.

Immediately, he glows red, and flies off to another part of the green.
Back in the ball room, save for Dr. Ver-Man and a few animals, it is now completely empty.

The skunk, the squirrels,
and a few other animals are all
that's left.

In addition, that
chimpanzee in his chauffer's hat
is playing the blues on a left-
behind sax.

In the doctor's mind, he
still keeps hearing those words,
in which Seandris had spoken to
him.

"You're weird." she echoes
in his mind.

He takes an angry deep breath.
With a remote control, he opens
a corridor behind a fancy curtain,
designed to cover a gigantic wall.
As the curtain moves aside, the
doctor enters that corridor with
his head hung low. It will take
him back to his underground lair.

He takes a picture of his
object of desire from inside his
ridiculed suit. He rips it to
shreds, by his shaken hands.

All the while, chaos continues
out on the course.

11

Everywhere he can, the Unstoppable Stopman fires his beams. They both pause the assortment of animals, and too knocks them back away from the party guest. He stops those animals especially that can cause severe harm.

No one is seriously hurt.

The QCPD are arriving in droves. Zookeepers are coming too.

Stopman then looks around, and sees that certain goose.

Stops watches that bird, as he flies into that well. The hero then follows that way.

Seandris beats helplessly at Andy Ape's rough exterior. Entering from yet another passageway, the gorilla now jumps upon a set of trees located within that underground jungle.

"Please, my family is rich." she pleads. "We can give you all that you want!"

At the same time, Malcolm has followed that squirrel down another long passage, which seems to be a dead end.

Hiding slightly, Malcolm notices the animal activating a door-sized passage that opens up to other hidden places. The squirrel enters, and the passage shuts behind the animal, and his acquisition.

Malcolm comes out of hiding.

He studies the "dead-end" for a moment. Then, he presses the same subtle button close to the floor, where the squirrel had been. It opens the passage.

As the authorities and zookeepers arrive and tend to the abundance of wild animals, the situation is pretty much under reasonable control. As stated, no one is seriously hurt. The club members and party guests are only offended that their best wardrobes are now fodder-looking.

"Only the animals love me." speaks the Dr. Ver-Man. He starts toward his underground, his sanctuary.

He's in a part of the lair that's full of irrigation and plant life. With each step, he goes further down in depth of his desired location.

Andy Ape continues carrying Seandris across the trees. She continues to scream.

Stopman hears her; for he is now flying amongst that underground jungle. Although he initially tries following the goose, he follows her screaming.

Meanwhile, Malcolm continues in the passage. Unafraid, he then suddenly hears a growl.

It freezes him in the dark.

In the dark, he sees beady reddish eyes coming towards him. Malcolm backs up.

A 400-pound bear emerges from the dark passage. Lucky for Malcolm, he finds a nearby corner. The bear runs past him. Yet, in addition to the bear come parrots, ducks, and an array of other animals, wild and domestic.

Andy Ape with Seandris on his massive shoulder dissents further down in that jungle.

"Put...me...down!" she insists.

The lady pokes and smacks at the gorilla's nose. He snorts, and puts her down upon a large tree branch. The ground is far down below. They are surrounded by jungle greenery.

Seandris faces the simian.

"Listen," she begins. "My family is not just rich...but wealthy. We'll give you anything!"
Just then, Andy Ape realizes he still has his mask on. He then removes it.

She screams, and begins to lose balance upon seeing Andy's true face.

She starts to fall. As Andy goes after her, the gorilla is hit with a red-beam. It causes the animal to fall off the branch roughly a long way down.

Seandris continues to fall too.

As she falls, Stopman flies directly under her. Then, he catches her.

Malcolm discovers the main part of the lair.

The moonlight above reveals the massive collection of priceless items. Gold, diamonds, money, and other items are piled up in this area.

12

"Wow!" exclaims Malcolm to himself. The amount of items could cost more than the country club above itself.

As Malcolm walks further into this underground, Malcolm hears something.

"Hey!" yells an overzealous police officer behind him. "Step away from the valuables, and put your hands up!"

Malcolm does as he's told instantly. Turning around, he looks the cop in the eye.

"Oh...please." mocks Malcolm. "Not much difference between a zoo and a country club, is it?"

Further away, Stops with Seandris in his arms lands her safely on the underground ground.

She exhales and pushes away from the crimson hero. With her eyes, she sizes him up.

"I'm curious." she begins. "Who *are* you?"

Stops is stoic. He has no clue how to respond. He just looks around; particularly at that "co-exist" banner ahead of him. Seandris's interest in him grows.

"You know, if you play your cards right you could get great fame."

     "I do not play cards, or play hero." Stopman explains to the lady. "I'm just trying to help."

     "And, you need to be thanked, somehow." she tells him.

     She approaches him.

     Stops just stands there, and she plants her lips upon his.

It is passionate enough to make other men jealous.

He is thrown a bit.

He tries to push her away, but she continues the kiss.

And then, emerging from the "Co-Exist" banner is Dr. Ver-Man. He immediately sees this embrace, with that raven on his shoulder.

The raven squaws loudly, flapping his wings.

It gets the attention of Stopman and Seandris.

The hero pushes her away. He then faces the doctor.

His eyes are wide with jealously. The eyes behind his bifocals rage red.

"So!" says Ver-Man angrily. " *This* is who the lady wants."

Stopman is inquisitive.

"Look citizen," he starts. "What is this place?"

The doctor just stands there, snarling.

Stopman starts to approach him.

Suddenly, from behind Ver-Man comes that honey-collecting beehive. It heads straight-on toward the hero.

Instinctively, the Stopman's red-beam surrounds him. Seandris just runs to the side, safely from the melee.

As Stops is preoccupied with the swarm now all over him, Dr. Ver-Man runs into the banner behind him. It comes down. In its place is more priceless stuff. More ominous is a giant sewage pipe, enveloped within a part of the stone caved wall.

Malcolm and that police officer arrive from afar. They join Seandris, who witnesses this confrontation.

"People keep telling me to *bee* myself." echoes a pun from the doctor. He turns toward that sewage pipe ready to walk the path it has seemingly set. Then, he starts walking towards it.

"But, in order to do that, I must *find* myself."

As Dr. Ver-Man walks into the sewage, the beehive starts to follow him. The bees upon Stopman's red-beamed shield begin to divorce themselves from the crimson-chrome crime-fighter. His beam around him starts to dissipate.

"Stopman!" yells Malcolm.

The bees have left Stops completely. Dr. Ver-Man is gone into that giant pipe.

Malcolm notices those stolen bearer bonds at his feet. He grabs them, while Stopman flies upward toward the moonlight that is past the open passage above.

Then, more police show up behind Malcolm, the first officer, and the beautiful lady.
Later on, the whole city would find out about this whole scenario.

The QCBC news reports that animal handlers have found some of the animals that had escaped from the zoo, and other places. Also, too the many valuables stolen all over Quad City have been mostly retrieved.

  After things are explained clearly, Malcolm is rewarded with an acquittal of his work-release sentence. The news even showed Stopman directing traffic, as more police arrived at the Quad City Country Club.

  During that whole situation and not a part of the news, that frightened maid made her way near a swampy pond.

She had, at this moment still been shaken, believing that what she had seen was a haunting.

Then, something rises out of that primordial muck. Covered in water weeds, with a white spherical piece where a mouth would be, is a figure shining in the moonlight.

This monstrous figure further scares this maid. She screams, and runs upon the country-club green.

The "monster" had removed the golf ball from his mouth (yes, a golf ball).

It is Paul Preppie.

He rubbed his head. His suit covered in mud and such. Apparently, Andy Ape's slap put him in that swamp.

"Ooooh my head." Paul says to himself.

He looks to the moon.

"I wonder if dad's got my mask." he says to himself. "The moon's perfect for a howl."

THE END

www.ingramcontent.com/pod-product-compliance
Lightning Source LLC
Chambersburg PA
CBHW071625030726

47598CB00001B/434